Pets RULE!

The Poodle
of Doom

Read all the  books

1

2

3

Get your paws on book #4, too!

The Poodle
of Doom

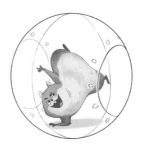

Written by
Susan Tan

Illustrated by
Wendy Tan Shiau Wei

SCHOLASTIC INC.

To Max, Oscar, and Beau: the best of poodles —ST

To Mom and Dad, thank you for always believing in me and encouraging me to do my best! —WTSW

Text copyright © 2022 by Susan Tan
Illustrations copyright © 2022 by Wendy Tan Shiau Wei

Library of Congress Cataloging-in-Publication Data

Names: Tan, Susan, author. | Wei, Wendy Tan Shiau, illustrator.
Title: The poodle of doom / by Susan Tan ; illustrated by Wendy Tan Shiau Wei.
Description: First edition. | New York : Scholastic Inc., 2022. | Series:
Pets rule; 2 | Audience: Grades 2-3. | Summary: Lucy's grandmother and her poodle Fluffy arrive for a visit, and Fluffy immediately begins building a doomsday machine that will hypnotize humans and turn them into agents of chaos—can Ember work with the other pets to outsmart this evil genius?
Identifiers: LCCN 2021036949 | ISBN 9781338756364 (paperback) |
ISBN 9781338756371 (hardcover)
Subjects: CYAC: Dogs—Fiction. | Pets—Fiction. | LCGFT: Novels.
Classification: LCC PZ7.1.T37 Po 2022 | DDC [Fic—dc23
LC record available at https://lccn.loc.gov/2021036949

10 9 8 7 6 5 4 3 2 1   22 23 24 25 26

Printed in China   62
First edition, October 2022
Edited by Rachel Matson
Cover design by Maria Mercado
Book design by Jaime Lucero

Table of Contents

Neo

Mr. Chin

Kevin

Fluffy

Steve

Ember

Mrs. Chin

Lucy & Poh Poh

The Chin Family ♥

CHAPTER 1

Doom Wears Pom-Poms

It was a beautiful morning in my kingdom.

I woke up on a soft pillow, next to my favorite human, Lucy. It had been a week since I arrived at the Chin family home. I already knew that soon this house, and then the world, would be *mine*.

I wagged my tail and barked evilly. Lucy giggled.

Then chaos struck!

Lucy's dad ran into her bedroom. "Lucy, hurry! We need to get the house ready! Poh Poh will be here any minute!" Mr. Chin yelled.

Poh Poh is Lucy's grandmother. I've never met her, but the other pets have. They like her.

"Oh, yay!" Lucy said. She leapt out of bed, got dressed, and ran downstairs to the kitchen. I followed behind her.

Downstairs, the humans were a *mess*. Mrs. Chin was running around sweeping. Mr. Chin was stuffing papers in drawers. Kevin was taking a smoking tray of muffins out of the oven.

The other pets—my minions—were already in the kitchen. I ran to join them. We had our own plans to make because there was a problem: Poh Poh wasn't coming by herself. She was coming with her poodle named Fluffy.

And according to the other pets, Fluffy was bad news. Or, in their words:

"Fluffy is PURE EVIL," Neo the canary chirped.

"He wants to DESTROY the world," BeBe the beetle called from Neo's back.

"Plus, he's just *mean*," Smelly Steve the hamster added.

I nodded like I agreed with them. But really, I wasn't so sure.

See, I am also evil. In fact, I'm a future Dark Lord. It's just that I want to *rule* the world, not destroy it.

4

I wondered what Fluffy would be like. I wondered if maybe I could convince Fluffy to work *with* me.

Maybe Fluffy was the key to my dark rule.

I opened my mouth to suggest this to the other pets.

Just then, Mrs. Chin came running by with a broom in her hand.

"She's here!" Mrs. Chin yelled.

Lucy ran to the front door.

She opened it, and there was Poh Poh.

"Lucy! Kevin!" Poh Poh yelled. She smiled.

"Poh Poh!" the Chins said, running toward her, burying themselves in a big group hug.

And just behind her, another figure stepped forward.

For a moment, all I could see was a giant shadow.

He was a towering figure, with pom-poms on his head, feet, and tail.

"Greetings, Fluffy!" I barked out. The rest of the pets cowered behind me. "I am Ember the Mighty, future ruler of this world! Together, we can do great things!"

I waited for his reply. My tail wagged. This was it, my new partner in evil!

Fluffy stepped forward. I could see his wide angry eyes and sharp teeth. I felt scared but also excited. What would Fluffy say? Would he be on my side?

"YOUR DOOM IS HERE!" he said. "BWAHAHAHAHA!"

CHAPTER 2

Not the Brownies!!

$\mathbb{T}$he Chins spent all morning talking and eating muffins. I stayed close to Lucy and avoided Fluffy. He was scary!

Then the Chins cleared the dining room table to make dumplings.

While they spread out flour and folded dumpling wrappers, Kevin told Poh Poh about how much he's been baking.

"Tonight, I'm making double-chocolate brownies," Kevin said. "I've already laid out the ingredients in the kitchen."

"Kevin's brownies are my favorite!" Lucy added. "He'll be a famous baker, I know it!"

Kevin grinned.

"And you will be a famous volcano scientist!" Kevin said.

"My grandkids. So talented," Poh Poh said.

"That reminds me," Lucy said. Her smile faded. "The school talent show is this week. I signed up to do a dance. But now I'm nervous."

"You'll be wonderful," Poh Poh said. "I can help! We'll make it the best dance. Then we'll celebrate with the almond cookies I bought." She nodded to a red box on the counter.

Lucy gave Poh Poh a flour-coated hug.

I tried not to be jealous of Poh Poh.

Normally, *I'd* be the one helping Lucy.

But I had other things to worry about. I had to get Fluffy out of the house.

Just then, I heard a noise.

Chiiiiiiiiirrrrrrppp!

It was Neo. That chirp was our signal. It meant that Fluffy was up to something!

"Over here," Steve whispered.

We crept into the kitchen, and my blood ran cold.

There, on the counter, were all the ingredients Kevin had put out for his brownies.

But Fluffy was pushing the bowl of chocolate chips toward the trash can. And in his paw, he held a bag of *RAISINS*.

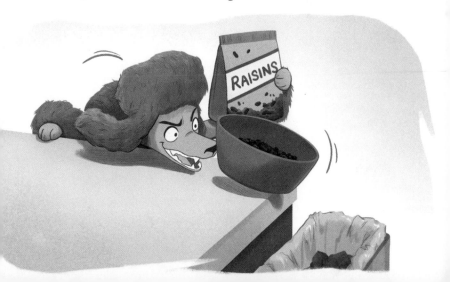

"Bwahahahahaaa!" Fluffy woofed. "I will replace this chocolate with raisins. The humans will blame each other for the mix-up! Chaos! DOOM!"

"Kevin's brownies!" Steve gasped.

"Lucy hates raisins! We have to stop him!" I shouted.

We raced forward. Neo grabbed Fluffy's ear with her claws. Steve attacked Fluffy's paw. I grabbed his tail.

We yanked Fluffy back from the counter. The raisins fell to the floor.

I looked around for a place to escape. The door to the laundry room was right behind us.

"Charge!" I yelled.

We crashed into the laundry room. I landed in a pile on top of Steve.

I jumped to my feet and faced Fluffy.

"Fluffy, I am evil like you!" I said. "Don't destroy the world! Rule it with me!"

"NEVER," Fluffy said. "Ever since our local dog park closed, I haven't gotten to play with other dogs. I don't have any friends! It's made me realize how terrible this world is. It must pay! You should be joining *me*! DOOM!"

I felt a twinge inside me.

As a future overlord of the world, I was a fan of evil.

And I was impressed by Fluffy. He had a *catchphrase*: something that only you can say.

But no. He'd tried to ruin Lucy's favorite brownies.

"I'll never join you," I barked.

Fluffy grinned an evil grin. "Fine. I will deal with you now, once and for all!" he said.

Fluffy raised his paw.

And I saw my doom.

CHAPTER 3

My Kingdom for a Dryer

Bwahaha! I will create chaos until the world is destroyed!" Fluffy declared.

Fluffy placed his paw on . . . THE DRYER.

I gasped. Steve backed away. Neo flew into the corner.

NO pets like the dryer.

But Fluffy, I saw in that moment, was not an ordinary pet. Fluffy was truly an evil genius.

Fluffy used his paw to turn a dial, and then . . .

WRRRRRRRRRR!!!

The dryer came to life!

"AAAAAAHH!" we yelled.

"BWAHAHAHAHAA!" Fluffy laughed.

We panicked.

"RUN!!" Smelly Steve shouted.

"Help!" Neo called.

"DOOM!" Fluffy woofed. Then he slipped out the door, back into the kitchen.

We tumbled out of the laundry room behind him.

"What on earth?" Poh Poh said.

The Chins were staring down at us, confused.

"Weird," Mrs. Chin said. "Why did someone start the empty dryer?" She went into the laundry room and turned the dryer off.

I rounded on Fluffy, who was standing behind Poh Poh.

"You are EVIL!" I cried.

"YES! And I shall DESTROY YOU ALL!" Fluffy shouted back.

"Aw, they're playing!" Mr. Chin said.

"You fool!" I barked at Mr. Chin. "The poodle will be your DOOM!"

Lucy looked concerned.

"Okay, I think that's enough playtime for tonight," Lucy said, picking me up gently. "I'll take Ember out. He's not that used to other dogs."

19

"Lucy, you have to believe me! Fluffy was trying to ruin Kevin's brownies," I woofed.

But she just kissed the top of my head. "Come on, puppy," she said.

After our walk, Lucy went to sit with Poh Poh in the living room. I stopped to drink some water and then went to join her. I looked into the room, and I FROZE.

Fluffy was sitting on the couch and curled up at LUCY'S SIDE. He grinned at me, showing sharp teeth.

I growled and backed out of the room. That was *my* spot on the couch!

I went upstairs to find Steve, Neo, and BeBe. They were regrouping in Lucy's room.

"See?!" Neo chirped. "That dog is EVIL."

"Yes," I said. I sank to the floor sadly. "An evil *genius*."

I couldn't lie. When we faced down Fluffy in the laundry room, for a moment I didn't know what to do. How could we defeat a dog who knew how to use the dryer?

But no.

I shook my head and stood up.

I was EMBER THE MIGHTY. No poodle would stand in *my* way or threaten *my* world.

"We will stop Fluffy at all costs!" I declared.

"Now you're talking," Steve said.

"YEAH!" Neo said.

"We will use his methods and learn to use the dryer and take over the world!" I said. "BWAHAHAHAHAAAAA!" I added an evil laugh, like Fluffy's. Tomorrow, I would work on a catchphrase.

It was time to think like Fluffy. It was time to show him that I was an evil genius, too.

Fluffy was about to meet his match.

CHAPTER 4

A Dog with a Plan

$\mathbb{T}$he next day, the Chins took Poh Poh to visit a museum. Fluffy stayed upstairs in Poh Poh's room all day. I wondered if he was making more evil plans.

The humans would be away for hours. It was time to gather the pets.

Neo and BeBe went to tell everyone we were meeting.

I waited for them out in the yard. Zar, a Russian wolfhound, was the first to arrive.

"Hi!" Zar boomed. Zar was big and impressive. He lived next door.

"Neo says there's an emergency," Zar said.

"Fluffy's back," Steve whispered. He rolled toward us in his plastic ball.

"FLUFFY! HIDE!" Zar yelled, diving behind Steve.

Zar was also scared of lots of things.

"Don't be afraid, Zar," I commanded. "With me in charge, we can take Fluffy down."

"Take who down?" a new voice asked.

I turned and gasped.

"AAAAH! A WALKING MOP!" Zar screeched.

An enormous, fluffy dog walked into the yard. "Actually, I'm an Old English sheepdog. My name's Izzy," she said.

"I invited her," Neo said. She flew in with BeBe on her back. "Izzy just moved here. Her human, Arjun, is in Lucy's class!"

I drew myself up. It was always good to have a new ally.

"I am Ember the Mighty, future ruler of the world," I said. "Will you help us save my kingdom from the forces of doom?"

"Oooh, forces of doom?" Izzy said. "I know JUST what to do."

"You do?" I asked. My tail wagged.

"Yeah! We'll have a DANCE-OFF!" Izzy shouted.

She struck a pose. My tail drooped.

"Uuuuhhh. I don't dance," I said finally. "Dark Lords don't dance."

"Well, I can also sing," Izzy said. "We'll have a sing-off! AaaaWHOOOOOOOOOOO!" she howled.

It was a terrible sound.

My fur stood on end. Zar hid under his paws. Neo fell from her perch. BeBe hid under Neo's wing.

"Let's save the singing for later," I said.

"Yeah, but you have an AMAZING voice!" Steve said.

We were getting VERY off track.

"All right," I barked. "FOCUS. To stop Fluffy, you must be my army."

"What does that mean?" Zar asked.

"It means," I said. "We TRAIN!"

They looked at me blankly.

"First, we'll practice commands. I'll say a command, and you'll follow it. Then we'll figure out how to use the dryer. Zar, I know the dryer scares you, but your height will be key," I said.

"Oh nooooo," Zar said. He hid again, this time behind BeBe. This worked even less well than hiding behind Steve.

"Listen, I think a dance-off might be easier," Izzy said.

"Yeah!" Steve said. "Look at this move!" He did a flip in his ball.

"Rock on!" Izzy said.

"Wait, no!" I said. "*I'm* giving the orders around here. And I say—"

"Look over there!" Neo gasped. "Everyone, it's Fluffy!"

We all turned. Fluffy was creeping toward the garden shed at the very back of the yard.

"What's he doing?" Steve asked.

"We have to follow him!" Neo said.

"*I* give the orders," I snapped. "But yes. Follow him!"

Neo frowned. But she followed me when I crept after Fluffy.

Fluffy snuck into the garden shed.

Zar boosted me up, and Izzy boosted Steve. We all looked through the dusty open window, into the shed.

We peered in. I gasped.

Doomsday had arrived.

CHAPTER 5

Spiders, Dogs, and Rock and Roll

$\mathbf{F}$luffy was building a machine.

The base was the Chins' old lawnmower. But now it was covered with wires, old socks, and held together with peanut butter.

And on the side, Fluffy had *labeled* his machine: *DOOMSDAY DEVICE. USE TO END THE WORLD!*

Fluffy didn't just know how to work the dryer. He could use *markers*.

We HAD to stop him.

"All right, we'll take this slowly," I whispered. "Fluffy can't know we're here until we strike. At my signal, Izzy—"

"ROCK OUT!!!" Izzy screeched. She charged through the door.

"ATTACK!!" Steve called, rolling in behind her.

"CHARGE!" Neo shouted.

"Noooo!" I yelled. But at this point, there was nothing to do but follow them in.

I raced through the door. I looked around. Maybe there was something I could use to destroy this evil machine!

But before I could find anything, Izzy ran up to Fluffy.

"Dance-off!" Izzy yelled. She began to shake her head back and forth to imaginary music. One of her wildly waving paws accidentally hit Steve's ball.

"STEVE!" I shouted. My loyal hamster was kicked *hard*. His plastic ball FLEW like it was one of Kevin's soccer balls.

"Heeeeeelllllp!" Steve cried. He flew straight out the door.

Zar screamed at the noise and went to hide under the workbench. This didn't work very well, because Zar was much bigger than the workbench.

"I'll get Fluffy, Ember!" BeBe called. She began to charge across the shed floor. Then she yelled, "Aaaah, a spider!"

A moment later, BeBe was running the other way as a small black spider came into view.

"Where's the party?" the spider yelled.

"I'll get Fluffy!" Neo called. She dove down, aiming for Fluffy.

Fluffy leapt to the side. Neo hit me instead, landing directly between my ears.

"OW!" I yelled.

I pulled myself dizzily to my feet. Our attack had failed.

I heard a chilling voice call out from behind me.

"You'll pay for this!" Fluffy cried. He lifted his paw.

BAM! Fluffy knocked over a rake.

"AAAAAH!" Zar yelled, panicked. He grabbed me by my collar and ran. We burst out of the door.

Our attack had been a DISASTER.

But little did I know that another, bigger disaster waited for me.

CHAPTER 6

A Dark Lord Alone

This is all your fault!" I yelled at the pets standing before me.

My army was assembled in the yard, and they were a sad group. Steve's ball was a little dented. Zar was cowering on the ground, and BeBe was resting on Zar's head. Neo's feathers were messy and covered with dust.

And me? I was ANGRY.

"I told you, we can only defeat Fluffy if you do *exactly* what I say," I said. "You have to obey all my commands! Izzy, you can NEVER rock out again, unless I tell you to."

"Oh. Okay," Izzy said, her ears drooping.

But suddenly, Neo flew up, chirping angrily.

"Says who?" Neo asked. She sounded fed up. "You know Ember, you're just as bad as Fluffy sometimes. You always boss us around."

"And you never ask us what we think!" Steve chimed in.

"And then you never say thank you!" BeBe added.

"Yeah, all I want to do is fetch, but you don't care! You just want me to do things that scare me, like face spiders and the dryer. That's not very nice!" Zar said.

"But . . ." I wasn't sure what to say. "But I'm your leader!" I said finally. "The future ruler of this world!"

"No, you're not," Neo said. "Not until you're nicer to us. Come on, everyone." She turned and flapped toward the house.

"Yeah, we'll make our OWN plan to save the world," Steve said, following her.

"And Izzy, you can rock out whenever you want," BeBe said, soothingly.

Together, they went back to the house.

"Wait!" I called after them. "No, you fools! This is what Fluffy wants! Obey me!" But none of them looked back.

I was left alone.

"I don't need my minions," I told myself.
"I can save the world on my own. And I can
take it over on my own, too!"

But I didn't feel that certain about it.

It was time to regroup. I knew just what
I needed to feel better: time with Lucy.
Maybe I could curl up on her pillow and
forget this had ever happened. I'd rest, and
then come up with a new plan, a way to
make everything better.

I went inside.

And walked straight into . . . A TRAP!

CHAPTER 7

The Great Almond Cookie Caper

$\mathbf{T}$he kitchen floor was covered in cookie crumbs. And not just any cookie crumbs. They were . . .

"My special almond cookies!" Poh Poh gasped.

I looked up. The Chins were back from their trip to the museum. I was standing in the middle of the kitchen, surrounded by crumbs. Right in my dog bed was the chewed-open box of almond cookies, the special ones Poh Poh had brought! It looked like I had eaten the cookies!

"It wasn't me," I barked.

"Bad dog!" Mr. Chin said.

"Oh, Ember." Lucy sighed. She looked sad. It was worse than anything that had happened that day.

"Wait, I can explain," I pleaded.

And then a dark figure came into the room. Fluffy grinned his evil grin. He leaned against Poh Poh's leg.

"It was him!" I yelled. "Look at the crumbs in his fur! I'm being framed."

I pointed toward him, and he *cowered*.

"That Chihuahua is a bully," Fluffy whined. He pretended to be *scared* of me.

I gasped. It was a terrible, evil plot. And it WORKED.

"Aw, poor baby!" Poh Poh said, kneeling down to hug Fluffy. "Is Ember being mean to you?"

"No, he's acting! He's fooling you all!" I shouted.

But nothing I said made any difference.

"Ember, BAD DOG," Mr. Chin said. "You'll be sleeping in the kitchen tonight."

Fluffy grinned again.

Lucy looked at me with sad eyes, but didn't say a word.

In that moment, I knew that Fluffy had won.

CHAPTER 8

A Poodle in the Night

I spent the rest of the day in the kitchen. I was trapped inside by a prison gate. I wasn't even allowed out to watch Lucy and Poh Poh practice the talent show dance. I heard Arjun come over to help choose the music, but I didn't even get to meet him.

I wanted to plot my revenge on Fluffy. But I felt too sad about what the other pets had said to come up with any brilliant ideas.

47

At night, Lucy scratched my ears and gave me a kiss on the head. Then she went upstairs. I was alone in the kitchen. A Dark Lord in the dark.

I was just starting to drift off when I heard strange noises.

BAM! CRUNCH! VROOM!

I bolted up. The sounds were coming from the garden shed!

I crept over to the porch door, which Mr. Chin always forgot to lock.

I tiptoed across the yard to the shed. A bright light shone from the window. I stretched as tall as I could to look inside.

But I couldn't see through the window on my own. I needed Zar to boost me up.

"No matter," I told myself. I tried not to think about how I'd yelled at Zar for being scared. Had I even said thank you for helping me attack Fluffy?

VROOM!

I heard the noise again.

I tiptoed to the door and nosed it open quietly, just enough so I could peer inside.

Fluffy was putting the finishing touches on his doomsday machine.

"Soon," he said to the machine, "I will use you to hypnotize and control the minds of everyone at the talent show. They will be my agents of chaos! And with them, I will destroy the world."

I gasped! Fluffy's plan was truly EVIL!

Fluffy whirled around, and something flew from his paw. A sticky mess hit me. I couldn't move! Fluffy had thrown a ball of peanut butter at me. My paw was glued to the ground!

Before I could do anything, Fluffy grabbed my collar.

Pop!

My paw came out of the peanut butter with a sticky sound!

Fluffy dragged me into the shed. "You think you can challenge me?" Fluffy demanded.

"I DO!" I shouted back. "This is *my* kingdom!!"

Fluffy walked closer to me. I backed up into a corner, where old boxes were piled high against the shed wall.

"It's *my* kingdom now," Fluffy said. "My machine is ready. And tomorrow at the talent show, everyone will know my genius. Unfortunately, *you* won't be there to see it."

Fluffy lifted a paw.

CRASH!

Fluffy hit the wall of old boxes. They fell and trapped me in the corner. I tried to move them, but they were so heavy!

"Goodbye, Ember the Not-So-Mighty!" Fluffy called.

I couldn't see anything but boxes. But I heard the sound of his machine clunking as Fluffy pushed it out the shed door.

And then he was gone.

I was alone, trapped beneath a tower of boxes.

I howled my anger.

But no one could hear me.

CHAPTER 9

Of Ghosts and Garden Sheds

I dug my way out of the tower of old boxes just as the sun was coming up.

I tried to open the shed door, but it wouldn't budge. Fluffy must have put something heavy in front of it.

I collapsed in a heap. Fluffy was right! I was Ember the Not-So-Mighty.

But then I remembered Fluffy's evil plan: He was going to unleash his doomsday device at the talent show today. Lucy was in danger!

I leapt to my feet. I had to do something!

I rammed my body against the door. I tried to pretend that I was Smelly Steve in his plastic ball, fast and unstoppable.

But the door wouldn't move.

Then I tried chewing at it, but that didn't do anything, either.

All I could do was howl. I tried to howl so loud and high that the windows would shatter. But nothing happened.

Then I heard voices from inside the house. The Chins were waking up! If I howled loud enough, they'd hear me. I would be saved.

But then I heard another sound. A sinister sound. The dryer!

Fluffy must have started it to drown out my noise. No one would hear me over that terrible sound.

I flopped to the floor, truly defeated. Fluffy had won. There was nothing I could do to protect Lucy. I was stuck here in this dark shed, covered in spiderwebs.

I looked around and shivered. I saw what Zar didn't like about scary places. I didn't like being here. I didn't like being all alone.

Suddenly, everything felt very dark. It felt like at any second, the shadows could leap out and get me. I worried that at any moment, I'd see a ghost.

I made myself into a small ball. I was okay. It would be okay. There were no such things as ghosts.

And then, out of nowhere, a voice spoke!

"Hello, stranger," the whispery voice said. "What brings you to my garden shed?"

CHAPTER 10

The Great Escape

"AAAH!" I jumped. Where was the voice coming from?!

"Over here!" the voice called. A tiny spider dropped from the ceiling.

"Hi! I'm Ari!" the spider said.

"Oh," I said. Suddenly, I wasn't very scared. "Nice to meet you. You startled me."

"Sorry! I don't get many visitors, apart from that other dog. I'm glad he's gone. His machine was LOUD!" she said.

"You have no idea," I said. "He has trapped me here. And he's going to hurt the Chins."

"Wait, BeBe's family?" Ari asked.

"You know BeBe the Beetle?" I gasped.

"She's my new friend! At first, she was scared of me. But I explained that I'm a friendly spider. Hey, I can go tell her that you're here!" Ari said.

I felt a wave of relief.

"Brave bug, if you help me escape, I will make sure that the world knows your name," I said.

"Cool!" Ari said.

I watched as she soared out the window.

Soon, I heard familiar voices. They were right outside the shed door.

"Ember!" Neo called.

"Neo!" I called back. I was so happy to hear her voice. "I'm stuck!"

"We're here to rescue you! Fluffy locked the door. I don't think any of us can open it! But we'll get you out," Neo said. A few minutes later, Neo flew through the window with an old jump rope in her beak.

"Okay, Ember, hold on to this," she said. I grabbed it with my teeth.

"Ready!" she called out.

"All right, Izzy," I heard Steve yell. "PULL!!!"

I felt a big tug. Suddenly, I was rising through the air.

Neo clamped her beak around my collar and flapped her wings to help me over the windowsill.

"Go, Neo!" BeBe cheered from Neo's back.

And then I saw Zar standing just outside the shed!

"Hop on, Ember!" Zar said. I stepped onto his giant head.

He lowered me gently to the ground.

I leapt off onto the grass. I looked around at them all.

I didn't know what to say. I was SO impressed. They were a really good team. And good at making plans, all on their own.

"I'm sorry!" I blurted out. "You were right. I was bossy. I don't want to be mean like Fluffy!"

"Thank you, Ember," Neo said.

"We missed you, Ember!" Steve and Zar said.

"You're cool, Ember," Izzy said.

I smiled at them all. My tail wagged in relief.

Then Neo sprang into the air.

"I almost forgot! Lucy has been frantic!" Neo said. "She searched for you all morning. But her parents finally convinced her to leave for the talent show. It starts in one hour!"

"Oh no!" I yelled. "We need to get to the talent show FAST to stop Fluffy's evil plan!"

I told them what Fluffy was going to do.

"How EVIL!" Steve gasped.

"Mrs. Chin and Poh Poh drove over in Poh Poh's car. And I saw Fluffy hide with the machine in the trunk, just before they left!" BeBe said. "Mr. Chin is about to drive over now."

"Wait, we should hide in *his* car!" Steve said. "Like Fluffy did!"

I opened my mouth to give a command. Then closed it.

"Great idea, Steve!" I said.

He grinned.

We ran to Mr. Chin's car and hid in the trunk just in time.

Mr. Chin drove to the school, and we went with him—to defeat Fluffy once and for all.

Dance, Dance, Resolution

Mr. Chin's car zoomed up to the school.

"Wheee!" Steve said as we pulled into the parking lot.

We waited for Mr. Chin to leave the car.

Then we tumbled out of the trunk and ran inside.

We followed signs for the talent show. The hallways were empty. Everyone was in the auditorium, getting ready for the show to start.

Suddenly, Izzy's nose began to twitch. "I smell peanut butter!" she said.

"It's Fluffy's machine!" I said.

"Follow me!" Izzy said. She began to run, and we followed behind her.

Izzy screeched to a stop at a door labeled BAND ROOM. It was right next to the auditorium.

We burst through the door.

The band room led right out onto the stage. And through the curtain, we could hear students singing. The talent show had begun!

Just then, there was a squeak of wheels, and Fluffy came into view. He had been hiding offstage. He was about to push his machine through the curtain and hypnotize the audience!

"We're too late!" Steve gasped.

What could we do? For once, I didn't have any ideas. I'd been a terrible leader, I hadn't listened to my friends, I . . .

MY FRIENDS.

All of a sudden, it hit me.

My friends had everything we needed to defeat Fluffy.

The things I'd seen as weaknesses were the things that made my friends *great*.

"I have an idea," I said. "If that's okay with you?"

"Go for it, Ember," Neo chirped.

"Okay," I replied. "Neo, Ari, BeBe, scout ahead and make sure no humans come this way! We can't risk them getting close to the machine."

"On it," Neo chirped. She zoomed out of the room.

BeBe and Ari cheered, "Go, Neo!" from her back.

"Izzy! Steve!" I shouted. "Rock and roll!!!!"

Izzy didn't hesitate.

"ROCK OUT!!" she howled. She began to dance. She kicked Steve in his plastic ball, just like in the shed.

"FOR THE CHINS!!!" Steve yelled. He flew through the air.

THUNK! His ball hit the center of the doomsday machine.

The machine fell over sideways. Peanut butter splattered everywhere.

"NOOOOOOOOOO!" Fluffy howled.

"Zar, fetch Fluffy!" I called.

Zar leapt forward. He grabbed Fluffy by the collar. Zar dragged him through the peanut butter, away from the stage door.

Steve, Izzy, and I rolled the doomsday machine into a closet.

"Rock out?" Izzy asked me.

"Great idea, Izzy," I said.

Izzy jumped on the machine, and rocked out a little more. As she danced, the machine crumbled and snapped. Peanut butter flew everywhere.

"My beautiful machine!" Fluffy whined as it fell apart. He fell, defeated, to the floor.

And I knew that we were safe.

We had stopped Fluffy once and for all. As a TEAM.

"My friends!" I woofed. "This is a great victory! You are all the best pets anyone could—"

"Ember!" Neo zoomed into the band room. "It's Lucy!!! She's in trouble!"

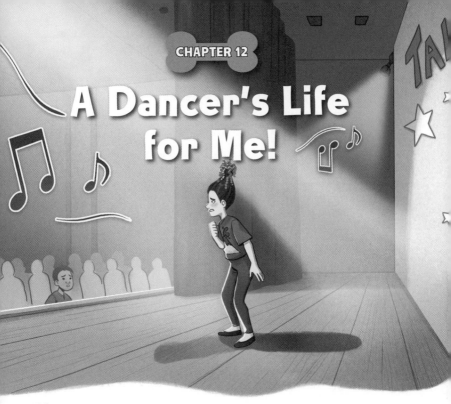

CHAPTER 12

A Dancer's Life for Me!

I ran to the stage and peered through the curtain.

Lucy was standing onstage, in front of the entire school. Music was playing, but she wasn't dancing. She was frozen.

"She was crying about you being missing just before she went on," Neo chirped in my ear. "Now I think she has stage fright!"

I saw Poh Poh in the audience, looking worried. She and Lucy had worked so hard on this dance!

I didn't think. I raced onto the stage.

"Ember!" Lucy said. "I was so worried."

I licked her ankle.

"There's no time, Lucy," I said. "You have a dance to do!"

And then I—Ember the mighty, future ruler of this world—began to *dance*.

I twirled. I pranced. I moved my ears to the music.

"Come on, Lucy," I woofed. "You can do it!"

Izzy raced onstage behind me.

"Yeah, Lucy," she woofed. "Rock out!"

"Come on, Lucy, you can do it!" Arjun said. He leapt from the audience and raced to the stage.

The music started playing. Lucy smiled and turned forward, and began to do her dance. It was the dance created by Lucy and Poh Poh. It was all about magma and volcanoes.

The dance ended and the auditorium CHEERED. Everyone was clapping for Lucy! I wagged my tail so hard I thought I'd fly off the stage.

"Come on, Ember," Lucy said, scooping me up. In the audience, I could see the Chins getting up to follow us.

Lucy took me into the band room.

Poh Poh came running in.

"I'm so proud of you, Lucy!" she said. "Let's celebrate! I found a place where we can buy almond cookies nearby!"

"And you," Poh Poh said, turning to me. "What a good dog! Though no more running away, okay?"

I licked her hand happily.

Then we all heard a sad "woof."

Fluffy was in the corner of the band room. He was covered in peanut butter, and half of a pom-pom was missing.

"Fluffy!" Poh Poh gasped. "WHAT ON EARTH HAVE YOU BEEN UP TO?!"

Poh Poh went over to scold him.

"I was so worried, Ember!" Lucy said. She cuddled me as the other pets gathered around.

"I know," I woofed. "But don't worry. With you by my side—" I paused. I looked out at the other pets. "With *friends* like ALL of you by my side, I know we can do anything."

The Chins drove us home. Mr. Chin kept saying, "BUT HOW DID THEY ALL GET HERE?!" But he seemed happy, too.

That night, we had a big dinner with Arjun and his parents, Mr. and Dr. Ramanathan. Lucy and Arjun were planning the next dance they'd create together. I was already thinking about joining in.

The humans ate dumplings and almond cookies, and Lucy fed me scraps from the table. Poh Poh told us that as soon as they got back to her house, Fluffy was going back to obedience school. Neo sang, perched on Mrs. Chin's chair, and Steve rolled around at Kevin's feet.

I watched them all happily. My kingdom. Just as it should be.

CHAPTER 13

New Beginnings

Poh Poh and Fluffy left after dinner—and after many hugs and scratches on my belly.

Fluffy looked quiet, but also happier.

"Good luck with obedience school," I said. "You know, I bet you'll make some friends there. Maybe now you can leave the world alone."

"We'll see," Fluffy woofed. But he sounded MUCH happier than he had before. I had a feeling that the world was safe from this particular agent of doom.

That night, I snuggled into Lucy's pillow. I was back where I belonged.

And now, my friends and I could get back to what was important: taking over the world. I knew that with all of us working together, we would come up with a plan in no time.

I was just falling asleep when a strange sound startled me awake.

Scratch! Scratch!

I jumped up. The noise was coming from just outside Lucy's bedroom window.

I got to my feet. I crept toward the window and put my face against it.

A pair of large, glowing eyes stared back at me.

"I have a task for you," a large orange cat whispered through the shadowy window. Her voice was low and mysterious. "If you prove yourself worthy, I'll give you your army . . ."

Susan Tan lives in Cambridge, Massachusetts. She grew up with lots of small dogs who all could rule the world. Susan is the author of the Cilla Lee-Jenkins series, and *Ghosts, Toast, and Other Hazards.* She enjoys knitting, crocheting, and petting every dog who will let her. Pets Rule! is her first early chapter book series.

Wendy Tan Shiau Wei is a Chinese-Malaysian illustrator based in Kuala Lumpur, Malaysia. Over the last few years, she has contributed to numerous animation productions and advertisements. Now, her passion for storytelling has led her down a new path: illustrating children's books. When she's not drawing, Wendy likes to spend time playing with her mix-breed rescue dog, Lucky. The love for her dog is her inspiration to help this series comes to life!

Pets RULE!

The Poodle of Doom

Questions & Activities

Ember is jealous of Fluffy's catchphrase. What is it? What do you think Ember's catchphrase should be?

How do Ember's friends feel after the failed attack on Fluffy? Why do you think they feel this way?

Reread page 50. What is Fluffy's plan to destroy the world?

Steve, Neo, Zar, BeBe, and Izzy all have their own special strengths. What are they? How do the friends combine their strengths to defeat Fluffy?

Lucy creates a dance for the talent show about her favorite thing, volcanoes. Create your own dance about YOUR favorite topic!